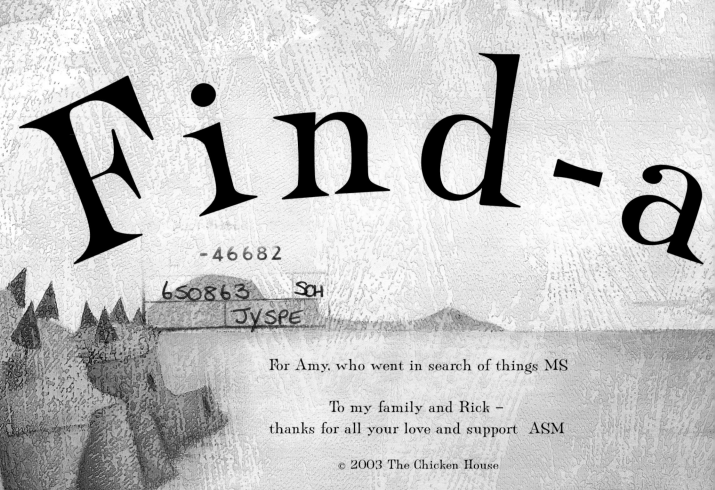

Find-a

For Amy, who went in search of things MS

To my family and Rick –
thanks for all your love and support ASM

© 2003 The Chicken House

First published in the United Kingdom in 2003 by
The Chicken House, 2 Palmer Street, Frome, Somerset, BA11 1DS
www.doublecluck.com

Text © 2003 Mark Sperring
Illustrations © 2003 Alexandra Steele-Morgan

Designed by Ian Butterworth

Printed and bound in China

British Library Cataloguing in Publication data available
Library of Congress Cataloguing in Publication data available

ISBN: 1 903434 91 2

By Mark Sperring

Saurus

Illustrated by
Alexandra Steele-Morgan

The Chicken House

One day Marty's mum started
to tell him all about dinosaurs.

Marty said he wanted to go for
a stroll with a Stegosaurus . . .

have burger and chips with a Brachiosaurus . . .

. . . and watch TV with a Tyrannosaurus!

Marty's mum explained that dinosaurs had lived a very long time ago and now, she was sorry to say, there weren't any left.

"There must be some dinosaurs somewhere." Marty sniffed. "I think they're just good at hiding."

The first thing he did when they got
back home was to look under the bed . . .

. . . but there was only a
silly monster hiding there.

Next he tipped up the laundry basket
. . . and out tumbled some elves.

He found a dodo
in the bathroom cabinet.

And an alien hiding under the table.

Up in the attic he found a
SOMETHING-OR-OTHER and a
THINGY-ME-JIG . . .
which wasn't what he
was looking for at all!

There was a sea monster hiding in the lilypond.

And a unicorn hiding in the garden shed.

Then he found an enormous footprint . . . .

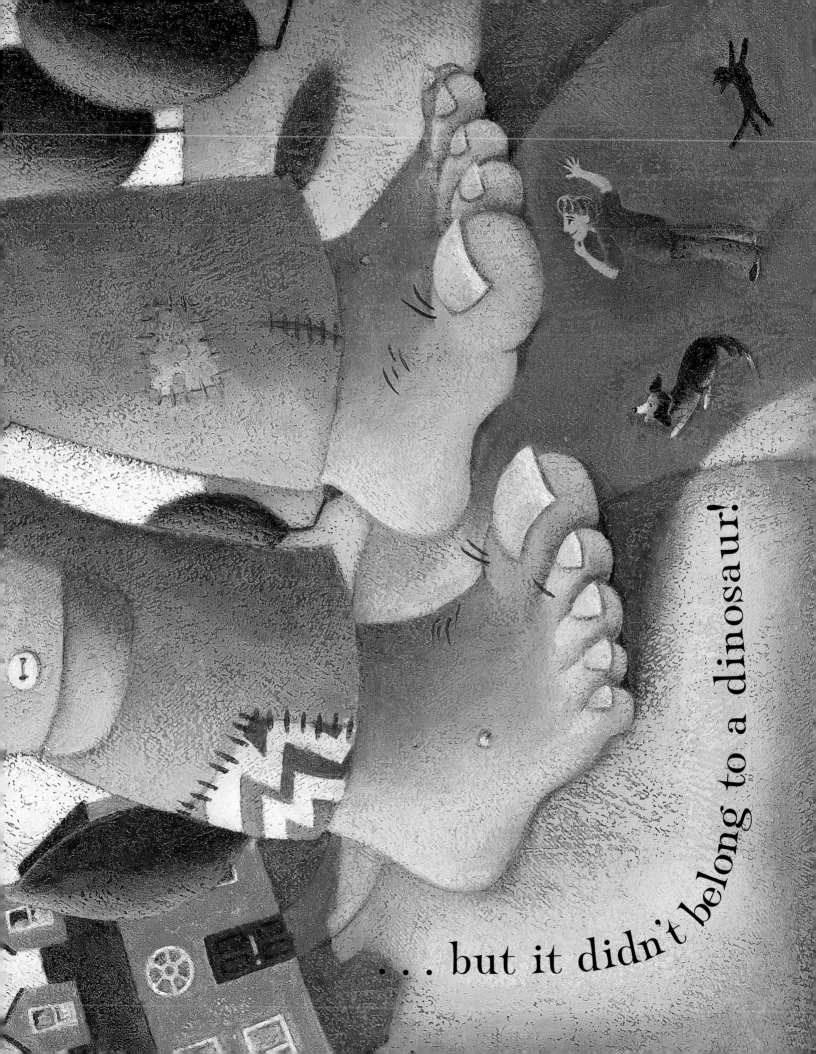

. . . but it didn't belong to a dinosaur!

He had looked in all the places he could think of
and he hadn't found one single 'Saurus.

"Mum, I've found a
dinosaur in it's hiding
place!" he cried as
he gave the tail a
mighty tug . . .

... but ...

Then he suddenly saw something
poking out of the toy cupboard. . . .

"Oh bother . . .
it's only a dragon!"

His mother explained all over again about dinosaurs. She talked and talked and read from book after book until she was sure Marty understood.

"I've changed my mind about
dinosaurs being good at
hiding," Marty said finally.
"They are BRILLIANT at it!"

"But one day I'll find one . . .
I just know I will!"